Toni Morrison
& Slade Morrison

THE TORTOISE OR THE HARE

ILLUSTRATED BY
Joe Cepeda

A Paula Wiseman Book
SIMON & SCHUSTER
BOOKS FOR YOUNG READERS
New York London Toronto Sydney New Delhi

To Nidal and Safa
—T. M.

To Kali
—S. M.

For Julian: May you find truth at the end of all your races
—J. C.

SIMON & SCHUSTER BOOKS FOR YOUNG READERS
An imprint of Simon & Schuster Children's Publishing Division • 1230 Avenue of the Americas, New York, New York 10020
Text copyright © 2010 by Toni Morrison and Slade Morrison • Illustrations copyright © 2010 by Joe Cepeda
SIMON & SCHUSTER BOOKS FOR YOUNG READERS is a trademark of Simon & Schuster, Inc.
For information about special discounts for bulk purchases, please contact Simon & Schuster Special Sales
at 1-866-506-1949 or business@simonandschuster.com.
The Simon & Schuster Speakers Bureau can bring authors to your live event. For more information or to book an event,
contact the Simon & Schuster Speakers Bureau at 1-866-248-3049 or visit our website at www.simonspeakers.com.
Also available in a Simon & Schuster Books for Young Readers hardcover edition
Book design by Laurent Linn
The text for this book is set in Tyfa. • The illustrations for this book are rendered in oil paints.
Manufactured in China • 0820 SCP
First Simon & Schuster Books for Young Readers paperback edition May 2014 • 10 9 8 7 6 5
The Library of Congress has cataloged the hardcover edition as follows:
Morrison, Toni.
The tortoise or the hare / Toni Morrison and Slade Morrison ; illustrated by Joe Cepeda. — 1st ed.
p. cm.
"A Paula Wiseman Book."
Summary: Jamey Tortoise is smarter than anyone else and Jimi Hare is faster, but when
a race is announced each consults a reporter about how to get what he really wants
when and if he should win in this updated twist on the familiar fable.
ISBN 978-1-4169-8334-7 (hardcover)
[1. Fables. 2. Folklore.] I. Morrison, Slade. II. Cepeda, Joe, ill.
III. Aesop. IV. Hare and the tortoise. English. V. Title.
PZ8.2.M673Tor 2010
398.2—dc22
[E]
2009047247
ISBN 978-1-4169-8335-4 (pbk)
ISBN 978-1-4424-3962-7 (eBook)

Jimi Hare couldn't help himself. He ran faster than anybody, everybody, everywhere. No one, not anyone, anywhere could beat him. He didn't know why his legs were made that way, or why his muscles were so powerful, but that's the way he was.

Everyone in the neighborhood avoided him.

Because he always won, they said he was no fun.

They called him

show-off, stuck-up,

too rough, too soft,

stupid know-it-all,

so slick, too quick,

a trick! A trick!

So Jimi ran alone.

Jamey Tortoise couldn't help himself. He was smarter than anybody, everybody, everywhere. Nobody anywhere could out-think him. He didn't know why his mind was so fast or his intelligence so high.

Everyone in the neighborhood
avoided him. Because he was so
smart, they said he had no heart.
They called him

stuck-up, show-off,

too rough, too soft,

stupid know-it-all,

selfish do-it-all,

so slick, too quick,

a trick! A trick!

So Jamey studied alone.

One day the newspaper announced
a contest. The winner of the race would
receive a golden crown.

Jimi Hare and Jamey Tortoise
both signed up.

Jimi practiced.

Jamey planned.

Jimi exercised.

Jamey strategized.

Jamey knew he was too slow to beat Jimi, so he called the newspaper and offered them an interview. When he spoke to the reporter, he said, "I know 'race' means 'fast' and 'win' means 'first.' But what story pleases your readers the most: the winner who loses or the loser who wins?"

"Oh," said the reporter, jumping up and down. "They are both wonderful stories. The loser who wins makes us all happy. But for overall satisfaction, it's when the winner loses."

"I see," said Jamey. "I know what you mean."

Jimi also called the newspaper and sat down with the reporter. "I know 'race' means 'fast' and 'win' means 'first,' but what gets the most attention: the largest crowd or the loudest cheers?"

"Oh, they're both important," she said, jumping up and down. "Loud cheers excite all of us. But for overall satisfaction, it's the largest crowd."

"I see," said Jimi. "I know what you mean."

At dawn on the day of the race, crowds lined the streets, and just as the reporter said, the large crowd got much attention. Signs and banners waved from windows and balconies. Some cheering; some jeering.

Then the starting flag dropped. Jimi began to run and entertain the crowd with leaps and somersaults and glorious stunts while Jamey crept slowly to the bus stop.

All day Jamey Tortoise
went from bus to train

to boat to plane.

All day Jimi Hare danced and ran and invented new stunts to please the crowd.

At last the sun set. The photographer
and the reporter waited at the finish line.

Jimi Hare arrived first.

Jamey Tortoise arrived second.

Since the reporter knew the story of the Tortoise and the Hare, she expected Jamey Tortoise to win. The next day there was a double headline in the newspaper:

WINNER LOSES! LOSER WINS!

"I won the race," said Jimi.

"I have the crown to prove it."

"I won the race," said Jamey.

"I have the headline to prove it."

It's not the race.

It's not who wins.

It's when the runners become good friends.